BY IRIS HISKEY ARNO
ILLUSTRATED BY JOAN HOLUB

Troll

*For moms I love—my mother, Miriam;
my grandmother, Esther; and my
mother-in-law, Edith
—I.H.A.*

*For Julie Hannah and Marjorie Hallowell,
two wonderful moms
—J.H.*

This edition published in 2001.

Published by WhistleStop, an imprint and registered trademark of Troll Communications L.L.C.

Printed in the United States of America. ISBN 0-8167-4440-8

20 19 18 17 16 15 14 13 12 11

I LOVE YOU, MOM

My mother is an artist.
There's paint on all her clothes.
And sometimes when she hugs me tight,
It rubs off on my nose.

Her pictures are gigantic,
And colorful—*wow-wee!*
The one that is my
favorite
Is of my dog and me.

My mom's an opera singer.
She travels far and wide.
When she's onstage
across the world,
I miss her deep inside.

But when I hear her singing,
It makes me feel so proud.
She looks so tall and beautiful,
And, boy, can she sing loud!

My mom is a beautician.
She'll cut or curl your hair,
And make you feel so beautiful,
You'll nearly walk on air.

But Mom says to remember,
What's inside counts for more.
For even if your outside's great,
You still could be a bore!

My mom is a scientist.
She knows the greatest things—
Like if a tree is old or young
By counting up its rings.

She knows what rocks are made of,
And she even wrote a book.
But when she comes home late at night,
She's glad my dad's the cook!

My mom's a cabinet maker.
She'll build you anything—
A bunk bed or a rocking horse,
A jungle gym or swing.

All week she's in the wood shop,
But weekends she's with me.
I'm learning how to build a fort
Out in our maple tree.

My mama works on race cars.
The line goes rushing by.
She tightens up the bolts so fast,
Her fingers nearly fly.

When we go to the racetrack,
My mama is the star,
Because her nimble hands
have worked
On every winning car!

My mother is a surgeon.
She helps fix injuries.
She operates on back and necks,
On shoulders and on knees.

She's worked on famous athletes,
But she would never boast.
My dad says you can see she's good—
Just watch her carve a roast.

My mom's a ballerina.
She twirls and she pliés.
Her partner lifts her in the air,
And people throw bouquets.

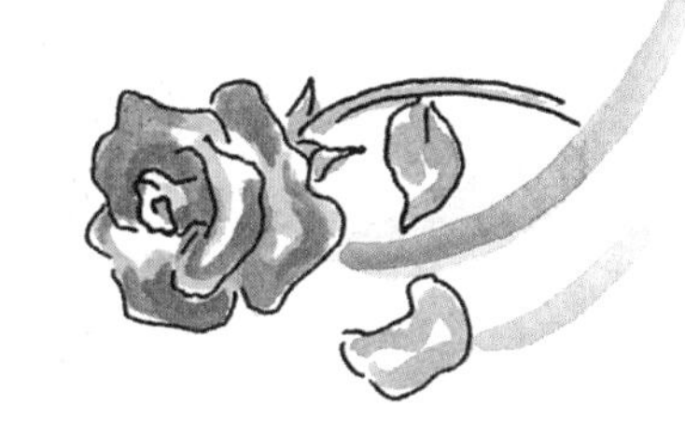

She makes it look so easy
To dance upon her toes.
But when I try to do it,
I fall right on my nose!

My mama raises kids.
She's got us four so far.
When we go to the shopping mall,
We nearly fill the car.

My mom can bake a cake,
Or fix a torn screen door.
And when it's time to give out hugs,
She's always got one more!

My mom's a cookbook author,
A tasty thing to be,
'Cause all the food she writes about,
She first cooks up for me!

She writes about tortillas,
Chow mein, and things like that,
And when she writes another book,
I know we'll both get fat!

My mom delivers letters.
She drives a big mail truck.
She says she hopes she brings good news
And happiness and luck.

And when she's been
out driving
In storms that rage and roar,
I like it when she comes
home safe
And walks through our
front door.

My mommy waits on tables
In Leroy's Coffee Shop.
She carries trays of steaming food
And never spills a drop.

When she comes home each evening,
My father rubs her feet.
And we put dinner on her plate
And tell her, “Have a seat!”

My mom's a trial lawyer.
She goes to court each day.
She cross-examines witnesses
And knows just what to say.

When I need a defender,
My mom is always there.
She shows me how to work things out
And makes sure that it's fair.

My mother's in the circus.
She swings on the trapeze,
And juggles balls and clubs and rings,
And does it all with ease.

And at my birthday party,
She dressed up like a clown.
And then she was the funniest
Of all the moms in town!

Every mom's a worker,
With talents that are great.
Each and every one's unique.
They're really all first rate!

One thing they have in common
Is kids like me and you,
Who love them and are very proud
Of all the things they do!